# HANNAH

---

A MODERN TALE OF LOVE AND FAITH

WOMEN OF THE BIBLE FICTION
BOOK 4

KAYLA LOWE

Want a free book? Sign up to my newsletter to get my award-winning book for free! www.authorkaylalowe.com

# MORE OF MY BOOKS

### Series

### Charms of the Chaste Court

A Courtship in Covent Garden
Whispers in Westminster
Romance in Regent's Park
Serenade on Strand Street
Treasure in Tower Bridge

---

### Sweet Honey by the Sea

The Beekeeper's Secret (Book 1)
A Royal Honeycomb (Book 2)
Bees in Blossom (Book 3)
Honeyed Kisses (Book 4)
Blooming Forever (Book 5)

---

### Strawberry Beach Series

Beachside Lessons (Book 1)
Beachside Lessons (Book 2)
Beachside Lessons (Book 3)

Panama City Beach Series

Sun-Kissed Secrets (Book 1)
Sun-Kissed Secrets (Book 2)
Sun-Kissed Secrets (Book 3)

The Tainted Love Saga

Of Love and Deception (Book 1)
Of Love and Family (Book 2)
Of Love and Violence (Book 3)
Of Love and Abuse(Book 4)
Of Love and Crime (Book 5)
Of Love and Addiction (Book 6)
Of Love and Redemption (Book 7)

Standalones

Maiden's Blush

Poetry

Phantom Poetry
Lost and Found

# CHAPTER 1

Hannah's gaze drifted from the flickering computer screen to the framed photo on her desk—a candid shot of her and James, their smiles radiant with hope and possibility. The image seemed to belong to another lifetime, a world untouched by the weight of their shared longing. She clicked through the endless stream of baby announcements and gender reveals, each one a bittersweet reminder of the joy that remained just beyond her grasp.

A knock at the door pulled her back to the present. "Hannah, the meeting is starting in five minutes," her assistant reminded her gently.

"Thank you, I'll be right there," Hannah replied, her voice steady despite the tempest brewing within. She straightened her blazer, a suit of armor against the well-meaning inquiries and sympathetic glances that awaited her in the conference room.

As she navigated the labyrinth of cubicles, Hannah's thoughts drifted to the appointment she and James had scheduled for that afternoon. Another round of tests, another glimmer of hope to cling to in the face of mounting disappointment. She silently recited a prayer, a plea for strength and guidance, as she took her seat at the long table.

The meeting passed in a blur of sales projections and market analyses, the numbers dancing before her eyes like distant constellations. Hannah forced herself to focus, to contribute, to prove that she was more than the sum of her unfulfilled desires. She felt James's absence keenly, longing for the reassuring warmth of his hand in hers.

Hours later, they sat side by side in the waiting room, the sterile white walls closing in on them like an arctic landscape. James's leg bounced nervously, a staccato rhythm that echoed the pounding of Hannah's heart. She reached for his hand, intertwining their fingers, a silent affirmation of their unbreakable bond.

The doctor entered, his expression a carefully crafted mask of professional detachment. "I'm sorry," he began, the words hanging heavy in the air. "The latest round of treatment was unsuccessful."

Hannah felt the room tilt, the ground shifting beneath her feet. James's grip tightened, anchoring her to the present. "What are our options?" he asked, his voice strained but resolute.

As the doctor outlined the next steps, the slim chances, and the mounting costs, Hannah felt a wave of exhaustion wash over her. The weight of their shared struggle, the countless prayers whispered in the dark, the dreams deferred and the plans put on hold—it all seemed to coalesce in that moment, a burden too heavy to bear alone.

Yet, as they walked out of the clinic, hand in hand, Hannah felt a flicker of something else—a quiet resilience, a stubborn hope that refused to be extinguished. She leaned into James, drawing strength from his steady presence, and together they stepped out into the uncertain future, their faith a guiding light in the gathering darkness.

The next morning, Hannah stepped into the office, her heart still heavy from the previous day's news. She made her way to her desk, the familiar bustle of the workplace washing over her. She immersed herself in her work, finding solace in the routine, the tasks at hand offering a temporary reprieve from the turmoil within.

Miriam's voice cut through the hum of activity, drawing everyone's attention. "Guys, I have an announcement to make!" Her face was radiant, her eyes sparkling with unbridled joy. "I'm pregnant!"

The room erupted in a chorus of congratulations, colleagues swarming around Miriam, offering hugs and well wishes. Hannah felt a sharp pang in her chest, a bittersweet mixture of happiness for her friend and a profound sense of loss. She plastered a smile on her face, joining the throng of well-wishers.

"Congratulations, Miriam," Hannah said, her voice wavering slightly as she embraced her colleague. "I'm so happy for you."

Miriam beamed, her hand instinctively resting on her still-flat stomach. "Thank you, Hannah. It's been such a journey, but we're thrilled."

Hannah nodded, swallowing past the lump in her throat. She knew all too well the weight of that journey, the endless cycles of hope and disappointment. As the conversation shifted to due dates and baby showers, Hannah quietly excused herself, slipping away to the sanctuary of the restroom.

In the harsh fluorescent light, Hannah gripped the edges of the sink, her knuckles turning white. She stared at her reflection, the woman looking back at her a stranger—hollow-eyed and fragile. The tears came then, hot and fast, spilling down her cheeks in silent rivulets.

"Why, God?" she whispered, her voice barely audible over the hum of the ventilation. "Why does it have to be this hard?"

She closed her eyes, drawing in a shuddering breath. In the stillness, a small voice seemed to whisper back, a gentle reminder of the faith that had carried her this far. *Trust in My plan, even when you cannot see the path ahead.*

Hannah let the words wash over her, a balm to her aching soul. She wiped away her tears, straightening her shoulders. She knew the road ahead would be difficult, the pain of this moment just one of many she would have to endure. But she also knew that she was not alone, that her faith and the love of those around her would be her strength.

With a final glance in the mirror, Hannah stepped out of the restroom, ready to face the day ahead. The weight of her struggle was still there, but so too was the flicker of hope, the unshakeable belief that somehow, someday, her prayers would be answered.

# CHAPTER 2

The clink of silverware against porcelain plates echoed through the dining room as Hannah and James sat across from each other, an unspoken tension hanging in the air between them. Hannah's gaze flickered from her husband's face to the untouched food on his plate, a sigh escaping her lips. They had been trying for so long, praying each month that this would be the one, only to have their hopes dashed time and time again. The weight of their struggle pressed down on her shoulders, threatening to suffocate the very life from her soul.

"How was work today?" James asked, his voice strained as he attempted to steer the conversation away from the elephant in the room.

Hannah's fork stilled, her eyes meeting his. "It

was fine," she replied, her tone flat. "But I think we need to talk about--"

"I've been meaning to tell you about this new project we're working on," James interjected, his words tumbling out in a rush. "It's a sustainable housing development that could really make a difference in the community."

Hannah's heart sank, disappointment washing over her. How could he not see that this wasn't about work? That the very foundation of their family, their future, was crumbling beneath them? She set her fork down, her appetite vanishing. "James, please. We can't keep avoiding this."

A heavy silence fell between them, the weight of unspoken words and unfulfilled dreams pressing down like a physical presence. James's jaw clenched, his gaze dropping to his plate as he pushed the food around with his fork. Hannah watched him, her own frustration and pain simmering just beneath the surface.

Later, as they sat on the couch, the flickering light of the television casting shadows across their faces, the distance between them seemed to stretch on for miles. Hannah hugged a pillow to her chest, her eyes fixed on the screen but seeing nothing. James sat beside her, his body rigid, his attention seemingly focused on the show. But Hannah knew better. She could feel the tension radiating off of him, the unspoken anger and helplessness that mirrored her own.

How had they come to this? She wondered, her heart aching with the weight of their shared pain. They had always been each other's rock, their love a steadfast anchor in the storms of life. But now, as they faced the greatest challenge of their marriage, it felt as though they were drifting apart, lost in a sea of their own grief and frustration.

Hannah's fingers tightened around the pillow, her eyes burning with unshed tears. She wanted to reach out to him, to bridge the gap that had grown between them. But the words wouldn't come, stuck in her throat like shards of glass. And so they sat, two hearts beating in the same room but separated by an ocean of unspoken pain, each silently praying for a miracle that seemed further out of reach with each passing day.

Hannah's phone vibrated, pulling her from the depths of her thoughts. She glanced at the screen, seeing Sarah's name flash across it. With a sigh, she rose from the couch, murmuring a soft "excuse me" to James before slipping into the kitchen for privacy.

"Hey, Sarah," Hannah answered, her voice barely above a whisper. "Thanks for calling."

Sarah's warm, nurturing tone enveloped her like a comforting embrace. "Of course, sweetie. I could tell from your text earlier that you needed to talk. What's going on?"

The dam broke, and Hannah found herself pouring out her heart to her best friend. She spoke of the growing distance between her and James, the way their once unshakable bond seemed to be crumbling under the weight of their fertility struggles. She confessed her fears, her doubts, and the overwhelming sense of inadequacy that haunted her every waking moment.

Sarah listened patiently, her gentle hums of understanding and empathy punctuating Hannah's words. When Hannah finally fell silent, Sarah's voice came through the line, soft but fierce with conviction. "Hannah, listen to me. You and James, you're both hurting right now. But you can't let this tear you apart. Your love, your faith, it's stronger than this."

Hannah closed her eyes, a single tear slipping down her cheek. "I know, but it's just so hard. I feel like I'm failing him, failing us."

"You are not failing anyone," Sarah insisted, her tone leaving no room for argument. "This is a journey, and it's okay to stumble along the way. But you need to lean on each other, and on God. He has a plan for you, even if you can't see it yet."

Hannah drew in a shaky breath, Sarah's words washing over her like a balm. "You're right. I know you are. It's just...it's so easy to lose sight of that when everything feels so dark."

"I know, honey. But that's why you have to take care of yourself, too. You can't pour from an empty cup." Sarah's voice softened, filled with understanding. "Make time for the things that bring you joy, that help you feel closer to God. Whether it's prayer, or journaling, or just taking a walk in nature. You need to nurture your own soul, so you can be there for James and for yourself."

Hannah nodded, a small smile tugging at her lips despite the tears that still flowed. "Thank you, Sarah. I don't know what I'd do without you."

"That's what best friends are for," Sarah replied,

and Hannah could hear the smile in her voice. "I'm always here for you, no matter what. And remember, God is too. Lean on Him, and trust in His plan. You and James, you'll get through this together. I know you will."

As the call ended, Hannah took a deep, steadying breath. The weight on her shoulders felt a little lighter, the path ahead a little less daunting. With Sarah's words echoing in her heart and her faith burning bright within her, she squared her shoulders and stepped back into the living room, ready to face the challenges ahead, hand in hand with the man she loved and the God who had never let her down.

# CHAPTER 3

The morning light filtering through the stained glass windows cast a kaleidoscope of colors across the pews as Hannah and James settled into their seats. The church was filled with the soft murmur of the congregation, a gentle hum that seemed to vibrate with anticipation.

As the service began, Hannah felt a sense of calm wash over her, the familiar rhythms of the liturgy soothing her troubled mind. She glanced at James beside her, his strong profile etched with a quiet reverence as he listened intently to Pastor John's words.

"In times of trial and hardship, it is easy to lose sight of God's plan for us," Pastor John intoned, his voice rising with conviction. "But it is in these moments that we must cling to our faith, trusting that He will guide us through the darkness and into the light."

Hannah felt the words resonate deep within her, a flicker of hope igniting in her chest. She had been grappling with the weight of her struggles for so long, the pain of infertility leaving her feeling lost and alone. But here, in the sanctuary of the church, surrounded by the love and support of her community, she felt a glimmer of that hope return.

As the service drew to a close, Hannah remained seated, her head bowed in silent prayer. James squeezed her hand gently before rising to join the others filing out of the church. Hannah barely noticed his absence, so lost was she in her own thoughts.

"Lord," she whispered, her voice trembling with emotion, "I know that you have a plan for me, even if I cannot see it now. I have struggled for so long, yearning for the blessing of a child. But I know that your love is infinite, and that you hear the cries of my heart."

Tears streamed down her face as she poured out her soul, the words tumbling from her lips in a torrent of raw emotion. "If you see fit to bless me with a child, I promise to dedicate their life to serving others, to raising them in your love and grace. I surrender myself to your will, trusting in your guidance and strength to carry me through whatever lies ahead."

As she finished her prayer, Hannah felt a sense of peace settle over her, a quiet assurance that somehow, everything would be alright. She rose from the pew, taking a deep breath as she stepped out into the sunlight, ready to face whatever challenges lay ahead with renewed faith and hope.

As Hannah stepped out of the church, a gentle breeze caressed her face, carrying with it the sweet fragrance of blooming flowers from the nearby garden. The warmth of the sun embraced her, its golden rays a tangible reminder of the divine presence that surrounded her. For a moment, she closed her eyes, allowing herself to be fully immersed in the tranquility of the moment.

A soft smile graced her lips, a stark contrast to the tears that had streaked her face mere moments ago. Though her circumstances remained unchanged, Hannah felt an inexplicable sense of peace, as if a heavy burden had been lifted from her shoulders. The weight of her struggles seemed to dissipate, replaced by a newfound lightness in her heart.

As she made her way down the stone path leading away from the church, Hannah's mind wandered to the sermon she had just heard. Pastor John's words echoed in her mind, a gentle reminder to trust in God's plan, even when the path ahead seemed uncertain. She marveled at the way his message had resonated so deeply within her, as if it had been crafted specifically for her ears.

Lost in thought, Hannah barely noticed the vibrant colors of the flowers that lined the path, their petals dancing in the gentle breeze. The world around her seemed to shimmer with a new brilliance, as if reflecting the renewed hope that blossomed within her heart. Each step she took felt lighter, imbued with a sense of purpose and determination.

As she reached the end of the path, Hannah paused, turning to gaze back at the church. The majestic structure stood tall against the azure sky, its stained-glass windows glinting in the sunlight. A wave of gratitude washed over her, a silent thanks for the sanctuary it had provided, both physically and spiritually.

With a deep breath, Hannah turned her face towards the future, ready to embrace whatever lay ahead. Though the road may be long and winding, she knew that she would face it with unwavering faith and the love of those who surrounded her. For now, in this moment of newfound peace, she allowed herself to simply be, basking in the warmth of the sun and the promise of brighter days to come.

# CHAPTER 4

The phone trembled in Hannah's hand as the doctor's words echoed in her mind. Pregnant. After years of heartache and dashed hopes, the impossible had become a miraculous reality. Tears of joy streamed down her face, glistening in the afternoon sunlight that filtered through the office window.

She placed a hand on her abdomen, marveling at the tiny life growing within her. In that moment, the world seemed to still, as if holding its breath in reverent anticipation. Hannah closed her eyes, whispering a silent prayer of gratitude to the heavens above.

As the initial shock subsided, an overwhelming urgency to share the news with James consumed her thoughts. She gathered her belongings, her movements fluid and purposeful, propelled by an energy she had not felt in months. The journey home passed in a blur of vibrant colors and muted sounds, her mind singularly focused on the precious secret she carried.

Hannah entered their home, her heart pounding in her chest. James looked up from his work, his brow furrowed with concern as he took in her flushed cheeks and bright eyes. "Hannah, is everything alright?" he asked, rising to meet her.

She took his hands in hers, her voice trembling with emotion. "James, I have something to tell you," she began, her words weighted with the gravity of the moment. "I'm pregnant."

Time seemed to suspend as James processed her words, his expression shifting from confusion to disbelief, and finally, to pure, unadulterated joy. "You're...we're going to have a baby?" he whispered, his voice thick with emotion.

Hannah nodded, tears flowing freely now. "Yes, my love. Our prayers have been answered."

James pulled her into a tight embrace, his own tears mingling with hers as they clung to each other, their shared sorrow giving way to an all-encompassing sense of hope and love. In that moment, the trials of the past faded away, replaced by the promise of a future filled with the laughter and love of the child they had so desperately longed for.

As they held each other, their hearts beat in unison, a testament to the unbreakable bond they shared. The journey ahead would undoubtedly be filled with challenges, but together, with their faith and love as a guiding light, they knew they could weather any storm. For now, they allowed themselves to bask in the warmth of this miraculous blessing, their hearts overflowing with gratitude for the tiny miracle that would forever change their lives.

The gentle tinkle of the coffee shop door chime heralded Hannah's arrival, drawing Sarah's attention from the well-worn paperback in her hands. As their eyes met across the cozy café, Sarah's face lit up with a radiant smile, the kind reserved for the dearest of friends. Hannah navigated the sea of tables, her steps light and purposeful, the weight of her secret news threatening to burst forth at any moment.

"Hannah, my dear!" Sarah exclaimed, rising to

envelop her friend in a warm embrace. As they settled into the plush armchairs, the rich aroma of freshly brewed coffee enveloping them, Sarah's keen gaze swept over Hannah's face, noting the barely contained excitement dancing in her eyes. "You're positively glowing! What's happened?"

Hannah reached across the table, grasping Sarah's hands in her own, the contact grounding her as the words she'd been longing to share tumbled from her lips. "Sarah, I have the most incredible news. After all this time, all the heartache and the prayers...I'm pregnant."

Sarah's eyes widened, her grip tightening as joyful disbelief washed over her features. "Oh, Hannah!" she breathed, her voice trembling with emotion. "This is...it's a miracle. I'm so incredibly happy for you and James."

Tears of shared joy and relief flowed freely as the two women embraced once more, their laughter mingling with the gentle hum of conversation that filled the café. As they settled back into their seats, Sarah's hand remained clasped in Hannah's, a tangible reminder of the unbreakable bond they shared.

"Tell me everything," Sarah urged, her eyes

sparkling with anticipation. "How are you feeling? When did you find out?"

As Hannah recounted the story of the life-changing phone call and the emotional revelation to James, Sarah listened intently, her heart swelling with love and admiration for her friend's strength and resilience. In the face of countless obstacles and setbacks, Hannah's unwavering faith and determination had carried her through, and now, in this moment of pure, unadulterated joy, Sarah couldn't help but feel a sense of awe at the power of the human spirit.

Their conversation flowed effortlessly, punctuated by the occasional burst of laughter and the quiet sniffles of happy tears. As the afternoon wore on, the shadows lengthening across the café floor, Hannah and Sarah continued to bask in the warmth of their friendship and the promise of the new life that grew within Hannah.

In the midst of their shared celebration, Hannah's thoughts drifted to the journey that lay ahead, the challenges and triumphs that awaited her and James as they embarked on this new chapter in their lives. Yet, with Sarah by her side, a constant source of support and understanding,

Hannah knew that no matter what the future held, she would never have to face it alone.

As the day drew to a close and the two friends parted ways, their hearts full and their spirits lifted, Hannah couldn't help but feel a sense of profound gratitude for the blessings in her life. The road ahead might be uncertain, but armed with the love of her family, the support of her friends, and the unwavering strength of her faith, she knew that she could face anything that lay in store.

# CHAPTER 5

Hannah stood in the doorway of the spare bedroom, a hand resting gently on her growing belly. Soft light filtered through the sheer curtains, casting a warm glow on the bare walls and hardwood floor. James joined her, his presence a comforting anchor as they surveyed the empty space before them.

"It's perfect," Hannah whispered, her voice carrying a mix of awe and anticipation. The room held the promise of new beginnings, a blank canvas waiting to be filled with love and laughter.

James wrapped an arm around her shoulders, pulling her close. "It is. And we'll make it even more perfect together."

They stepped into the room, their footsteps

echoing in the stillness. James retrieved a paint swatch book from the windowsill, flipping through the pages of soothing hues. Hannah's eyes lingered on a delicate shade of sage green, its calming essence resonating deep within her soul.

"This one," she said softly, pointing to the color. "It reminds me of new growth, of hope."

James nodded, a smile playing at the corners of his lips. "Sage green it is. We can add some accents in cream and soft yellow, create a peaceful oasis for our little one."

As they discussed furniture and decor, their earlier struggles seemed to fade into the background. Laughter filled the room as they playfully debated the merits of different crib designs and changing tables. In these moments, the weight of their journey lifted, replaced by the simple joy of creating a space for their long-awaited child.

Hannah felt a fluttering in her belly, a gentle reminder of the life growing within her. She placed James's hand on her stomach, watching his eyes widen in wonder as he felt the tiny kicks. In that instant, their connection deepened, a shared reverence for the miracle they had been blessed with.

Days turned into weeks as the nursery took shape. Soft green walls embraced a white crib adorned with delicate lace bedding. A plush rocking chair sat in the corner, inviting moments of quiet bonding. Shelves lined with treasured books and stuffed animals waited patiently for tiny hands to explore their wonders.

Hannah ran her fingers along the smooth wood of the changing table, marveling at the transformation of the once-empty room. It had become a sanctuary, a tangible expression of their love and dedication. Each carefully chosen item held a piece of their hearts, a testament to the strength of their bond.

As the nursery neared completion, Sarah appeared at their doorstep, her eyes sparkling with excitement. "I have a surprise for you," she announced, guiding Hannah and James to the living room where a gathering of loved ones awaited.

Pastel streamers and balloons adorned the space, their soft colors mirroring the serenity of the nursery. A table overflowed with thoughtfully wrapped gifts, each one a symbol of the support and love that surrounded them.

Hannah felt tears prick the corners of her eyes as she took in the smiling faces of her friends and family. Their presence was a balm to her soul, a reminder that she was not alone in this journey. Sarah embraced her tightly, whispering words of encouragement and love.

As the baby shower unfolded, Hannah found herself enveloped in a cocoon of warmth and affection. Laughter mingled with heartfelt conversations, creating a tapestry of shared joy. Each gift she unwrapped held not only practical necessities but also the promise of cherished memories to come.

In the midst of the celebration, Hannah's gaze drifted to James, their eyes locking in a moment of quiet understanding. They had weathered storms together, their love growing stronger with each challenge faced. Now, as they stood on the cusp of parenthood, their hearts swelled with gratitude for the blessings that had brought them to this moment.

As the sun began to set, casting a golden glow through the windows, Hannah knew that whatever lay ahead, they would face it together. Their love, their faith, and the unwavering support of those around them would guide them through the joys and trials of their new chapter. And in the nursery down the hall, a room filled with hope and promise awaited the arrival of their precious child, a testament to the power of perseverance and the indomitable strength of the human spirit.

The soft glow of the moon cascaded through the nursery window, casting a gentle light upon Hannah as she sat in the rocking chair, her hand resting on her swollen belly. The room was still, save for the gentle creaking of the chair as it swayed back and forth, a soothing rhythm that mirrored the beating of her heart.

In the quiet of the night, Hannah's thoughts drifted to the promise she had made to God, the words etched into her soul. She closed her eyes, remembering the desperation and longing that had consumed her in those moments of prayer, the plea for a child to call her own.

Now, as she sat in the room that would soon welcome their little one, Hannah felt a wave of gratitude wash over her. The journey had been long and arduous, filled with moments of doubt and sorrow, but through it all, her faith had remained steadfast.

"Thank you," she whispered, her voice barely audible in the stillness of the room. "Thank you for hearing my prayers, for granting me this precious gift."

The words flowed from her lips, a heartfelt prayer of thanksgiving and devotion. She promised to raise her child in love and faith, to guide them along the path of righteousness, and to always remember the miraculous way in which they had come into the world.

As she spoke, Hannah felt a sense of peace envelop her, a warmth that seemed to emanate from within. It was as if God's presence filled the room, wrapping her in a comforting embrace.

With each passing moment, Hannah's resolve grew stronger. She knew that the road ahead would not be without its challenges, but she was ready to face them head-on. Her love for her unborn child, her unwavering faith, and the support of her husband and loved ones would be her guiding light.

As the night wore on, Hannah remained in the nursery, her whispered prayers a testament to the depth of her devotion. And when at last she rose from the rocking chair, her hand lingering on the crib that would soon cradle her child, she knew that no matter what the future held, she would always keep her word to God, cherishing the miracle of life that had been entrusted to her.

# CHAPTER 6

The shrill cry pierced the air, a triumphant herald of new life emerging into the world. Hannah collapsed back against the pillow, chest heaving, as the final wave of pain receded. Beside her, James gripped her hand tightly, his eyes wide with wonder and awe.

"You did it, my love," he whispered, pressing a gentle kiss to her sweat-dampened brow. "Our son is here."

As if on cue, the nurse approached, cradling a squirming bundle swaddled in soft white. With infinite care, she placed the newborn into Hannah's waiting arms. The weight of him, solid and warm against her chest, stole Hannah's breath. She gazed down at the tiny face, marveling at the delicate features—the rosebud mouth, the fluttering eyelids, the wisps of downy hair. In that moment, the struggles and heartaches of their journey fell away, eclipsed by a love so fierce it threatened to consume her.

"Hello, Samuel," Hannah murmured, her voice thick with emotion. "We've been waiting for you."

James leaned in close, one arm encircling his wife while the other hand reached out to stroke the baby's cheek with a trembling finger. His eyes shone with unshed tears, reflecting the depths of his own overwhelming emotions. In this sacred space, where the veil between heaven and earth seemed gossamer thin, he felt the weight of the divine—a palpable presence bearing witness to their joy.

Hannah's heart swelled as she watched her husband's awestruck expression, the tenderness in his gaze a mirror of her own. Together, they had weathered storms and clung to hope when the darkness threatened to engulf them. Now, in the quiet hush of the hospital room, they basked in the light of this new beginning, their love forged stronger through the trials they had endured.

Samuel stirred, his tiny hand breaking free of the blanket to curl around Hannah's finger. She marveled at the strength in that miniature grip, a tangible reminder of the life they had created. James pressed a gentle kiss to the baby's downy head, his touch a silent promise of protection and guidance.

As Hannah cradled her son close, she felt a profound sense of purpose settle over her—a calling that transcended her own desires and dreams. This child, entrusted to their care, was a gift beyond measure. With each breath he took, each flutter of his eyelids, she knew that her life had been irrevocably changed. The path ahead would be filled with both joy and challenge, but armed with faith and fortified by love, she knew they would navigate it together.

In the golden glow of the room, the little family cocooned in a moment outside of time, Hannah's heart whispered a silent prayer of gratitude. For this day, for the miracle in her arms, and for the man by her side who had walked through the valley of shadows with her. Together, they had emerged into the light, their love a testament to the unwavering power of hope and the unbreakable bonds of family.

The morning light filtered through the stained-glass windows of the church, casting a kaleidoscope of colors across the faces of the congregation. Hannah and James stood at the altar, their infant son cradled in Hannah's arms, his tiny form swathed in a white christening gown that had been passed down through generations of their family.

Pastor John, his kind eyes crinkling at the corners, smiled warmly at the young couple. "We gather here today," he began, his voice resonating through the hushed sanctuary, "to dedicate Samuel to the Lord, and to celebrate the miraculous journey that brought him into this world."

As the pastor spoke, Hannah's mind drifted to the promise she had made in the depths of her despair—a vow to dedicate her child to God if He would only grant her the blessing of motherhood. Now, standing before her church family, she felt the weight of that promise settling upon her shoulders, a mantle of responsibility and love.

James, sensing her emotion, reached out to clasp her hand, his touch a steadying anchor amidst the swell of feeling. In his eyes, she saw the reflection of her own joy and trepidation, the acknowledgment that they were embarking on a sacred trust.

Pastor John's voice washed over them, his words a balm to their souls. "Let us pray for this child, that he may grow in wisdom and grace, and that he may always know the love of his Heavenly Father."

As the congregation bowed their heads in prayer, Hannah felt a profound sense of peace descend upon her. The journey that had brought them to this moment had been marked by struggle and doubt, but through it all, their faith had been a guiding light, illuminating even the darkest of paths.

With trembling hands, she handed Samuel to the pastor, watching as he gently cradled the infant, anointing his forehead with holy water. "Samuel," he intoned, his voice filled with reverence, "I baptize you in the name of the Father, the Son, and the Holy Spirit."

A hush fell over the sanctuary, broken only by the soft coos of the baby. In that moment, Hannah felt the presence of something greater than herself, a love that transcended earthly understanding. She knew, with a certainty that reached to the very core of her being, that Samuel was a child of God, destined for a purpose beyond their imagining.

As the pastor placed the infant back in her

arms, Hannah looked out at the sea of faces before her—the friends and family who had walked beside them, offering prayers and support in their time of need. In their eyes, she saw the reflection of God's love, a tangible reminder of the blessings that had been bestowed upon them.

With a heart full to bursting, Hannah turned to James, their eyes meeting in a moment of perfect understanding. Together, they had weathered the storms of life, their love and faith a beacon in the darkness. Now, as they stood on the threshold of a new chapter, they knew that they would face whatever lay ahead with the same unwavering commitment, their hearts bound by a love that could move mountains.

# CHAPTER 7

Hannah stood in the doorway of the nursery, her eyes fixed on the tiny form of her son nestled in his crib. The soft glow of the night light cast a warm halo around his cherubic face. James walked up behind her, his steady presence a comforting anchor in the sea of emotions that swelled within her heart.

"Sometimes I still can't believe he's really ours," Hannah whispered, her voice trembling with a mix of awe and gratitude. "After everything we went through..."

James wrapped his arms around her waist, drawing her close. "I know. But we made it, together. Our little miracle."

They stayed like that for a while, two silhouettes against the backdrop of the nursery, their shared love for their son binding them even closer. The struggles of the past seemed distant now, like fading echoes drowned out by Samuel's gentle breathing.

In the days that followed, Hannah found herself drawn to the church, a newfound purpose taking root in her soul. She approached the pastor with an idea, her words tumbling out in an earnest rush.

"I want to start a support group, for women facing infertility. To let them know they're not alone."

The pastor smiled, his eyes shining with understanding. "That's a wonderful idea, Hannah. I know your journey will inspire so many."

And so it began. In a cozy room within the church walls, Hannah sat in a circle with women of all ages, their faces etched with the same longing and pain she knew all too well. She shared her story, her voice wavering but never breaking, and watched as glimmers of hope rekindled in their eyes.

As the weeks passed, the group grew, each new face a testament to the power of shared experience. Hannah found solace in their stories, in the way they lifted each other up with words of encouragement and prayers whispered in unison. It was in this sacred space that she discovered a different kind of fulfillment—one born from the act of giving, of pouring her heart into the lives of others.

In the quiet moments, when she rocked Samuel to sleep or felt James' hand in hers, Hannah marveled at the tapestry of her life—the threads of sorrow and joy, of loss and love, all woven together into a picture of grace. And she knew, with a certainty that resonated in her very bones, that every step of her journey had led her here, to this place of purpose and peace.

The gentle breeze carried the sound of Samuel's laughter as he chased a butterfly across the lush green lawn. Hannah watched from the porch, a serene smile playing on her lips, her hands wrapped around a steaming mug of tea. The years had been kind to her, laugh lines etched around her eyes like a map of the joys she had experienced.

As she watched her son play, Hannah's mind drifted to the winding path that had led her here.

The pain of infertility, once a heavy weight on her heart, had slowly transformed into a source of strength - a reminder of her resilience and the unwavering love she shared with James.

Her thoughts turned to the women in her support group, their faces now as familiar as family. She remembered the tears they had shed together, the prayers they had whispered, and the triumphs they had celebrated. Each story, each journey, had become a part of her own, woven into the fabric of her being.

A contented sigh escaped her lips as Samuel ran towards her, his eyes sparkling with the care-free innocence of childhood. She scooped him up in her arms, breathing in the sweet scent of his sun-kissed hair. In that moment, Hannah felt a profound sense of gratitude wash over her, a deep appreciation for the winding road that had led her to this perfect moment.

"Mommy, look!" Samuel exclaimed, pointing to a butterfly that had alighted on the railing beside them. Its delicate wings shimmered in the sunlight, a reminder of the beauty that could emerge from even the most challenging of circumstances.

Hannah smiled, her voice soft as she whispered, "Isn't it wonderful, my love? Just like that butterfly, we've gone through a transformation, and look at the beauty that surrounds us now."

As the butterfly took flight, Hannah felt a sense of peace settle in her heart. She had found her purpose, not just in the love of her family, but in the way she had turned her pain into a beacon of hope for others. And in that realization, she knew that every moment, every struggle, had been a blessing in disguise, guiding her to this place of profound joy and contentment.

## EPILOGUE

The warm sunlight dappled through the leaves as Hannah sat on the park bench, watching James and Samuel in the distance. She smiled softly, her heart swelling with a love so profound it felt almost ethereal.

James knelt beside their son, his hands gently guiding the boy as he balanced on the small bicycle. Samuel's face was a picture of concentration, his brow furrowed and tongue poking out slightly as he focused on the task at hand.

"You're doing great, buddy," James encouraged, his voice carrying across the grass. "Just keep pedaling, nice and steady."

Samuel wobbled for a moment, but James's strong hands kept him upright. Slowly, tentatively, James released his grip, and Samuel began to pedal on his own. Hannah held her breath, a mix of pride and trepidation filling her chest as she watched her little boy navigate the path ahead.

As Samuel gained confidence, his face broke into a wide grin, laughter bubbling up from his small frame. James jogged alongside him, cheering him on with every turn of the pedals. Hannah felt tears prick at the corners of her eyes, a wave of gratitude washing over her.

Years ago, in this very park, she had poured out her heart to God, pleading for the miracle of motherhood. The journey had been long and arduous, filled with moments of doubt and despair. But through it all, her faith had been her anchor, a steadfast reminder that even in the darkest of times, hope persisted.

Now, as she watched her husband and son, their laughter mingling with the gentle rustling of leaves, Hannah felt a deep sense of peace settle within her. The path to this moment had been winding and uncertain, but it had led her to a love more profound than she could have ever imagined.

James caught her eye from across the park, his smile soft and knowing. In that moment, a silent understanding passed between them—a recognition of the trials they had faced and the strength they had found in each other.

Samuel pedaled back towards them, his cheeks flushed with exertion and joy. "Mommy, did you see me?" he exclaimed, leaping off the bike and into Hannah's arms.

She held him close, breathing in the sweet scent of his hair. "I did, my love. You were amazing."

James joined them on the bench, his arm wrapping around Hannah's shoulders. She leaned into his touch, feeling the steady beat of his heart against her own.

In the golden light of the afternoon sun, Hannah closed her eyes, offering up a silent prayer of thanks. For the gift of her family, for the strength that faith had given her, and for the love that bound them all together.

And as she sat there, surrounded by the two people she cherished most in the world, Hannah knew that no matter what the future held, they would face it together—a family full of love and hope, always.

Hannah stepped into the community center, her heart filled with purpose. The room was buzzing with the chatter of women from all walks of life, each seeking guidance and support. She smiled warmly, remembering the countless times she had longed for a mentor during her own struggles.

"Welcome, everyone," Hannah began, her voice soft yet confident. "I'm so grateful to have you all here today."

As she shared her story, the women leaned in, their eyes glistening with empathy and understanding. They nodded along, recognizing pieces of their own journeys in Hannah's words.

"I know how it feels to be lost, to question your faith when faced with seemingly insurmountable challenges," she continued, her gaze sweeping across the room. "But I'm here to tell you that there is always hope, even in the darkest of times."

The women murmured in agreement, their spirits lifting with each word Hannah spoke. She guided them through exercises and discussions, offering wisdom and encouragement at every turn.

As the session drew to a close, a young woman approached Hannah, her eyes brimming with tears. "Thank you," she whispered, clasping Hannah's hands in her own. "Your words have given me the strength to keep going, to trust in His plan for me."

Hannah embraced her, feeling the weight of the woman's gratitude settle in her heart. This was her calling, she realized—to be a beacon of hope for others, just as she had once needed herself.

In the weeks and months that followed, Hannah's mentorship program flourished. She watched as the women blossomed, their faith and confidence growing stronger with each passing day. And as she witnessed their transformations, Hannah felt a profound sense of fulfillment wash over her.

This was where she was meant to be—a mother to Samuel, a mentor to these women, and a servant of God. Every struggle, every tear, every prayer had led her to this moment, and she knew that she would never take it for granted.

For Hannah had learned that life's greatest blessings often came from its greatest challenges—and that with faith and love, anything was possible.

# EXCERPT FROM DEBORAH

The stage lights illuminated Deborah's face as she stepped up to the podium, her blue eyes scanning the audience of business leaders and professionals gathered before her. She took a deep breath, the weight of her message settling on her shoulders like a mantle of responsibility.

"Integrity," she began, her voice clear and commanding, "is the cornerstone upon which we must build our businesses, our communities, and our lives."

Deborah's words hung in the air, demanding attention and introspection from all who listened. She spoke of the temptations that come with power and success, the easy paths of compromise and corruption that could lead even the most principled astray. Yet, she reminded them, it was in these moments of choice that true character was forged.

As she spoke, memories of her own battles against unethical practices flashed through her mind—the long nights spent pouring over financial reports, the tense boardroom confrontations, the whispered threats from those who preferred the status quo. Each challenge had tested her resolve, but she had emerged stronger, more committed to her values than ever before.

"We are the guardians of our own integrity," Deborah said, her gaze sweeping the room. "It is a responsibility we cannot abdicate, a duty we owe to ourselves and to those who depend on us."

She painted a vision of a business world where honesty and fairness were not just platitudes but guiding principles, where success was measured not just in profits but in the positive impact made on lives and communities. It was a world she had fought for all her life and would continue to fight for, no matter the cost.

As her speech drew to a close, Deborah's voice grew softer, more reflective. "In the end," she said, "we will be judged not by our titles or our bank accounts, but by the content of our character. Let us strive every day to be leaders of integrity, in our businesses and in our lives."

The audience rose to their feet in a standing ovation as she stepped back from the podium, but Deborah barely noticed the applause. Her mind was already turning to the battles ahead, the injustices that still needed to be righted. She knew her work was far from over, but with conviction burning in her heart, she was ready to face whatever challenges lay ahead. For in the fight for integrity, there could be no retreat, no surrender - only the unwavering determination to do what was right, no matter the odds.

Boarded-up windows and "For Lease" signs adorned the once-vibrant storefronts along Main Street, a testament to the conglomerate's suffocating grip on the city's economy. The few pedestrians who braved the sidewalks moved with a sense of dejection, their shoulders slumped under the weight of an uncertain future. In the distance, the gleaming tower of the conglomerate's headquarters loomed like a modern-day citadel, casting a long shadow over the struggling neighborhood.

Deborah navigated her car through the potholed streets, her heart heavy as she witnessed the decay firsthand. The speech she had given at the conference seemed a distant memory now, her words of integrity and fairness ringing hollow in the face of such blatant exploitation. She tightened her grip on the steering wheel, a silent vow to herself that she would not let this injustice stand.

As she turned the corner, Deborah's eyes widened at the sight before her. A crowd had gathered outside the gates of a factory, their signs and chants demanding fair wages and job security. Police officers in riot gear formed a barricade, their batons at the ready. The tension in the air was palpable, a powder keg waiting for a spark.

Deborah pulled to the curb, her mind racing. She knew the factory well—it had been a pillar of the community for generations, providing stable employment for hundreds of families. Now, it seemed, it had fallen victim to the conglomerate's insatiable appetite for profit.

A man broke from the crowd, his face etched with desperation. "Please, Ms. Lawson," he pleaded, recognizing her from the news. "You have to help us. They're shutting down the factory, laying off everyone. We don't know what we're going to do."

Deborah's heart clenched at the raw emotion in his voice. She knew all too well the pain of losing one's livelihood, the fear of not being able to provide for one's family. In that moment, the path before her crystallized with a clarity that took her breath away.

"I will help you," she said, her voice steady with resolve. "I don't know how yet, but I promise you, I will do everything in my power to make this right."

The man's eyes glistened with unshed tears as he nodded his thanks. Deborah watched as he rejoined the crowd, their chants taking on a new fervor in the face of her pledge.

As she drove away, Deborah's mind churned with the enormity of the task before her. Taking on the conglomerate would be no easy feat—they had money, power, and influence on their side. But she had something more—the unshakeable conviction that what they were doing was wrong, and the determination to see justice served.

In the rearview mirror, the factory faded from view, but its image remained seared in Deborah's mind—a symbol of all that had been lost, and all that she would fight to reclaim. The road ahead would be long and fraught with challenges, but she knew in her heart that it was a journey she had to take. For the sake of the city she loved, and for the people who called it home, she would not rest until integrity and fairness reigned once more.

Deborah arrived at her office, her mind still reeling from the encounter with the community leaders. She sat at her desk, staring blankly at the reports and spreadsheets that awaited her attention. The numbers blurred together, losing meaning in the face of the real-life struggles she had just witnessed.

She leaned back in her chair, closing her eyes as she tried to process the weight of the responsibility now resting on her shoulders. The conglomerate's actions were not just unethical—they were causing tangible harm to the very fabric of the city. Families were being torn apart, livelihoods destroyed, and dreams shattered.

A knock at the door jolted her from her thoughts. "Come in," she called, straightening in her seat.

Her assistant, Lydia, poked her head into the

room. "Sorry to disturb you, Ms. Lawson, but there's a journalist here to see you. Says he has some information about the conglomerate that you might find interesting."

Deborah's pulse quickened. "Send him in."

A moment later, a man in his early thirties entered the office, a leather satchel slung over his shoulder. "Ms. Lawson, thank you for seeing me on such short notice. I'm Ben Fisher, with the City Chronicle."

She shook his hand, studying him closely. There was an intensity in his gaze that suggested he was more than just another reporter chasing a headline. "What can I do for you, Mr. Fisher?"

He reached into his bag, pulling out a stack of documents. "I've been investigating the conglomerate for months now, and I've uncovered some disturbing information. Bribery, corruption, environmental violations—it goes deep."

Deborah's eyes widened as she flipped through the pages, her heart sinking with each damning revelation. "This is...incredibly compelling evidence. With this, we might actually have a chance of bringing them to justice."

Ben nodded, a grim smile on his face. "I thought you might say that. I've heard about your reputation, Ms. Lawson. If anyone can take on this fight, it's you."

She met his gaze, a newfound sense of purpose crystallizing within her. "Thank you, Mr. Fisher. I promise you, I will not let this information go to waste. The conglomerate's days of operating with impunity are numbered."

As Ben left her office, Deborah felt a flicker of hope amidst the daunting challenge ahead. The road would be long and the opposition fierce, but armed with the truth and the support of those who believed in her, she knew that victory was possible. All that remained was to take that first step, and trust that God would guide her path.

Get Deborah: A Modern Tale of Love and Leadership now!

## ABOUT THE AUTHOR

Award-winning author Kayla Lowe writes women's fiction that explores complex themes with sensitivity and depth. Kayla's books delve into the intricacies of relationships, self-discovery, and resilience. From cozy love stories interspersed with a bit of faith to heartwarming tales of friendship and suspenseful novels of empowerment and heartbreak, her books illustrate the struggles specific to women.

When she's not churning out her next novel, you can find her with her feet in the sand and a book in her hand or curled up on the couch with her dogs.

Visit her website at www.authorkaylalowe.com.

**ALSO BY KAYLA LOWE**

<u>Series</u>

<u>Charms of the Chaste Court</u>

A Courtship in Covent Garden

Whispers in Westminster

Romance in Regent's Park

Serenade on Strand Street

Treasure in Tower Bridge

<u>Sweet Honey by the Sea</u>

<u>The Beekeeper's Secret (Book 1)</u>

<u>A Royal Honeycomb (Book 2)</u>

<u>Bees in Blossom (Book 3)</u>

<u>Honeyed Kisses (Book 4)</u>

<u>Blooming Forever (Book 5)</u>

---

<u>Strawberry Beach Series</u>

<u>Beachside Lessons (Book 1)</u>

<u>Beachside Lessons (Book 2)</u>

<u>Beachside Lessons (Book 3)</u>

---

Panama City Beach Series

Sun-Kissed Secrets (Book 1)

Sun-Kissed Secrets (Book 2)

Sun-Kissed Secrets (Book 3)

---

The Tainted Love Saga

Of Love and Deception (Book 1)

Of Love and Family (Book 2)

Of Love and Violence (Book 3)

Of Love and Abuse(Book 4)

Of Love and Crime (Book 5)

Of Love and Addiction (Book 6)

Of Love and Redemption (Book 7)

---

<u>Standalones</u>

Maiden's Blush

---

<u>Poetry</u>

Phantom Poetry

Lost and Found

www.ingramcontent.com/pod-product-compliance
Lightning Source LLC
Chambersburg PA
CBHW021347160726
47994CB00007B/2865